Strings of Love

By

Priyanka
Bhattacharjee

Noel Lorenz House of Fiction
www.noellorenz.com
India. Africa

Title of Book: **Strings of Love**
Author of Book: **Priyanka Bhattacharjee**
First Published in India in August 2022 by **Noel Lorenz House of Fiction**

ISBN 13: 978-93-93695-09-3

Published and Printed By
Noel Lorenz House of Fiction
Headquarters - Kolkata, West Bengal, India
154A, KCG Road, Kolkata - 700050
www.noellorenz.com

About the Book

SYNOPSIS: 'LOVE' -The most divine feeling that exists on Earth. Infact it is the string of love that ties all of us to eachother. But, we humans at times fail to realise this aesthetic feeling. Sometimes, we don't even realize how and in which form love comes into our life.

'Strings of love' is a book which will give you readers an insight to how important love is in our life. Love is not only about having attraction towards the opposite sex. It's more than that. Love has many forms. With a hope that the essence of love fills all your hearts, the author presents this book to you all.

- Priyanka Bhattacharjee

28th August 2022

Assam, India

About the Author

Priyanka Bhattacharjee who is born and raised in the beautiful land of tea gardens Assam, is an English teacher by profession and has an ardent love for English literature. Having a positive attitude towards life even in the most adverse situations is her sole motto.

Apart from teaching, she also loves cooking new recipes, listening to music and singing. But, what she loves the most is scribbling her emotions. She started writing since childhood but never thought to be published author. However, destiny had some other plans and today she is a co-author of around 20 anthologies and that too in a span of a year.

She has recently been awarded with best writer award by JEC Publication and has been winners of many poetry challenges conducted by NLHF and Ink Your Words.

'Strings of Love' is her dream project. It is her first book as a solo author. She hopes to be appreciated and encouraged for her endeavour.

Priyanka Bhattacharjee

Acknowledgements

I extend my heartiest gratitude to my mother from whom I inherited the skill of writing. I am also grateful to my father and my husband for their constant support and encouragement. Also thank you Lorenz Sir and NLHF for adorning me with this privilege. And thank you God for your continuous blessing.

Priyanka Bhattacharjee

Contents

THE AGELESS BOND

Sitting at her window sill, she gazes at the sun slowly vanishing away beyond the horizon. As she watches the sky changing its colour from the rich hues of red and orange into the darkness of the night, she can realize how the bright sun of her youth is slowly setting off.

She gets up and walks towards the mirror. She can see her youthful face lost behind the signs of ageing. Touching her face to feel the wrinkles, she sits in the recliner kept nearby and gets submerged into deep thoughts. She begins reminiscing her youth – when she led a carefree life filled with vigour.

A joyful girl she was, Lavanya – yes, her name which her parents kept after a lot of speculation meaning beauty and grace – she used to be the lifeline of her family. She was truly an epitome of beauty: both inside and out.

Lavanya was born in a middle-classed family. Her father was a government service holder which was a matter of pride not only for him but also his wife. Lavanya's mother was a simple housewife who didn't have any high expectations from life. She was happy with the fact that her husband had a job which gave her both security as well as respect. The salary Mr. Abani Mitra brought home was enough to fulfill their basic needs. A happy and contented life they had.

But, was Lavanya happy with her life? Since her childhood, she saw her father going to office every morning at 9 and returning home at 6 in the evening. Working as a clerk in PWD department he was so immersed in his files that he hardly had any time to notice his daughter growing or his wife's beautiful hair locks turning grey. Her mother too had molded herself in such a manner that she never demanded anything from Mr. Mitra. She had no complaints.

Lavanya doesn't remember a single family vacation when they went anywhere other than her grandmother's home. Her parents provided her with all her necessary amenities. But, never with anything, she could call a luxury. She was taught to be satisfied with whatever she got because there were many who were not even that lucky to have what she had. Although, she never spoke a word; but Lavanya knew what she wanted from her life.

Taking a trip down the memory lane, Lavanya dozes off at the window sill. The cool breeze flutters her hair and she is immersed in a deep sleep; when suddenly the doorbell rings which disrupts her peaceful slumber. She walks to the door but when she opens it, there is no one to be seen.

Lavanya gets irritated. This is not the first time. The children of the colony often did this to annoy her. She tried to catch them a couple of times. But couldn't. Once, she even got them, but they escaped. And with her growing age and osteoarthritis, she couldn't run after those impish kids to catch them.

She closes the door and sits back in her recliner. She lives alone. Kamala, her caretaker comes twice a day to do all the household chores. But, since last few days, Kamala is running high temperature due to which she couldn't come. Hence, Lavanya is alone. But, more than that she is lonely. She has nobody with whom she can have a heart to heart talk.

Nonetheless, this life was chosen by Lavanya herself.

Ma, I don't want to get married. Don't force me.

Every girl needs to get married my sweetheart. Even I got married.

And what have you achieved in life getting married? Except being confined within the four walls of this house.

This used to be the age-old argument at Mitra House. Lavanya never wanted to get married. She had seen her mother's turmoil throughout her life trying to please her husband and in-laws.

This wasn't the life Lavanya dreamt of. She wanted a good job that would pay her a handsome salary with which she could lead a life of luxury- the life she desired for herself and her family.

And Lavanya did achieve her dream. With her untiring hard work and dedication, she cracked the IAS Examination and with time was appointed the Deputy Commissioner. As promised to herself, she not only established herself but provided her parents with a life they never imagined of.

They were proud of the position their daughter had earned in the society. She proved her potentiality not only to her parents but to everyone who had ever doubted on her ambition. But, somewhere her parents were worried about her.

Lavanya, you have now achieved everything that you wanted in your life. You have given us a life we never dreamt of. But, we will always not be there for you. Now, it's time you get married. You are already in your thirties.

But Lavanya, by no means, wanted to enter the conjugal bond. She was happy with her life. She needed nobody in her life. She was happy with her parents.

But, no one lives forever. With time her parents passed away and she was left alone.

Today, when she looks behind; she realizes every word her mother said. Life truly can't be led alone. Tears rolled down her cheeks thinking of her parents when her mobile beeped.

Her bank account was credited with her first pension. But, this couldn't charge her mood. Money, luxuries and comforts of life which were once her priorities lost their significance now. What her heart now wants is someone whom she can call hers. She now wants true love that she shoved off years back.

Love did come her way once upon a time. But, she never appreciated it. There was a time when she not only had her loving parents but also a very good friend and colleague Satvik. They met each other during the time when Lavanya was posted to Alipurduar. It didn't take a long time for Satvik and Lavanya to be friends in spite of the fact that Satvik was her junior. She, being alone in Alipurduar, Satvik started taking a lot of care of her.

With time their bond grew stronger. For Lavanya, it was nothing more than pure friendship. But, Satvik was in deep love with her. He wanted her as his life partner.

Finally, he decided to propose her and one fine evening, he reached her quarter with a bouquet and a ring. He revealed his feelings for her and proposed for marriage. Lavanya remained silent for a while and then spoke.

Satvik, for me life had always been about achieving my dreams and living a free life. Love and marriage are never in my list. You were always my best friend. But, today you snatched away my friend. I have no intention of getting married ever. Neither today nor in the future. It's better we part our ways.

Twenty-five years passed since then. Lavanya never thought she would ever regret her decision. Today, in her lonely life she wants Satvik back. But, she knows it quite well that it's impossible. Satvik would have his family now and the kind soul he had been, he will obviously be a great husband and doting father.

Sitting in her recliner, as she looks back into her life, she realizes life is not only about earning money and position. Real happiness comes only when one has a companion with whom one can share the highs and lows of life. But, now it was too late. As goes the saying, *'Time and tide waits for none'*. If only she could have rewound her life, she would have rectified all her blunders. As she was lost in her thoughts, suddenly the doorbell rang.

Although reluctant, she gets up from her recliner and slowly drags herself to the door. As she opens the door, she stands there dumbstruck. She can't believe her eyes. There stands outside her door a man in his sixties and he is none other than her age-old friend- Satvik.

She is stunned. This is most unexpected.

Is there some kind of connection between us? Is this what people call telepathy? How could he be here? That too after so many years! Lavanya keeps thinking to herself when Satvik speaks up.

Will you not let me in? Can't you recognize me? I am your long forlorn friend Satvik. I came here for some work and thought to check if you are here. Must say, I am lucky enough to find you.

Lavanya comes into her senses and immediately calls him in.

Please be seated. It's such a pleasure to meet you after years. How are you?

Lavanya keeps gazing at Satvik. He still has that sparkle in his eyes. And his smile half hidden behind his French cut beard- it's to die for.

How could I never notice how attractive he is? His looks are to die for. Even at this age he still looks enticing.

Lavanya keeps mumbling to herself.

How's life, Lavanya? Satvik asks.

She wants to say that nothing is fine. Life after him was never the same. But she resists herself.

Everything is fine, Satvik. How are you?

I am fine too. You haven't changed Lavanya except your grey hair. You spent your life the way you wanted. Happily, single! Satvik grinned.

Yes, I am still the same. Happily, single. But, you definitely have your family.

You could never understand me, Lavanya. I loved you truly. And till today you are my only love. I never got married. I have always waited for you.

This is beyond Lavanya's expectation. She can't believe her ears. Tears roll down her eyes. How could she never realize how much Satvik loved her? But, it's better late than never. She decides to reveal what she feels for him.

Teary eyed Lavanya speaks,

Satvik, I had seen my mother sacrificing all her pleasures because my father could never afford them. She did that smilingly. Never complained. I could feel how she hid her desires behind her smile. But, I never wanted this for me. Hence, I decided never to get married. Little did I realise that with time my thoughts would change. Today, I have everything in my life. But, I am not happy. I regret my decision. Today I crave for companionship. I committed the biggest blunder in my life. I lost the best partner of my life.

What Satvik heard just now is unbelievable. This is what he wanted to hear since ages. He takes hold of Lavanya's hands and says,

You haven't lost me and you will never. I am always yours. I will be with you whenever you need me. I always wanted to marry you. But I respected your decision. Till today, I love you and want you in my life.

But Satvik, I am no more that young Lavanya you fell in love with once. I am no more beautiful. How can you love me now?

Lavanya, love is not about mere physical attraction. I didn't love you for your beauty but for that strong personality you always had been. I still love you for the human being you are. Marriage needn't be the

culmination of every relation. Let's remain as friends as we always had been.

Lavanya was overwhelmed. She was lonely no more. She got her friend back. Her respect for Satvik knows no bounds.

Truly, love is divine and beyond any definition. Lavanya tells to herself. She realizes now what kept her mother happy and content throughout her life.

A FRESH RESTART

"It's not working between us. Let's part our ways. It's better to be separated than to stay together and fight on every petty issue," said Karan to his wife Kavita.

Karan and Kavita are married now for ten years. But in these ten years, there is not a single day that they have spent without any argument. Karan liked nothing about Kavita. Actually, he never wanted to marry Kavita. She was never his choice.

Karan and Kavita were poles apart. Karan used to be the heartthrob of every girl during his college days. Enjoying life and living it to the fullest has always been his motto. He, still loves partying with his friends and enjoying outside.

Kavita, on the other hand, has always been a quiet girl. She never had many friends. Her interests are quite different from Karan. She loves staying at home, reading books and listening to music. She always wanted a calm and quiet life. However, she's an ideal daughter and now an ideal housewife.

So, how did these two completely contradictory personalities come together? Kavita and Karan's fathers were childhood friends. They were very close to each other. They were more like brothers than friends. When they had their children, they both promised to get them married so that their bond gets stronger. And that's how Karan and Kavita came together.

Since their marriage, Kavita had been putting efforts to satisfy Karan. But, nothing seemed to impress him. He always kept finding loopholes in whatever Kavita did. He kept rebuking her. Kavita was hurt but yet she tried to mend their relation. She loved him and wanted to have a happy family with him.

Kavita thought to talk to Karan.

"Karan, I know I am not the kind of girl you wanted to marry. Nevertheless, we are married now and we need to put efforts to make our marriage successful."

"I am neither interested in you nor in our relationship."

"But, I am Karan. I want our relation to work. Tell me what I should do to please you."

"Fine. You want to please me. I like nothing about you. Did you ever see your dressing sense? You don't even know how to talk to people. But I am ready to give you a chance. Tomorrow, it's my friend's birthday. He is going to throw a party. He has invited both of us. I shall take you with me. But you need to dress and behave the way I want."

Kavita agreed. That evening Karan bought her a dress to wear to the party.

In the morning Karan asked Kavita to be ready for the evening. When Kavita took out the dress, she saw it was a short dress. She had never worn such dress before. However, to please her husband she wore the dress. She tried to look the way Karan wanted.

Karan took her to the party. It's for the very first time Kavita attended such a party. She was uncomfortable. Yet, she tried to socialize with everyone there. Then Karan's friend offered her a glass of whiskey which she refused politely. Karan saw this and forced her to have it. Although, Kavita kept refusing, Karan forced her to have the drink. When Kavita didn't adhere to his will, Karan angrily dragged her from the party and took her home.

They had a big argument and then Karan told her that he wanted to get divorced. Kavita stood there in shock. She spent the whole night in tears.

Kavita woke up in the morning to see that Karan had already left for his office. Kavita planned to make up for the previous night. She cooked all his favorite dishes. She also ordered for a cake and a gift for him. It was evening and Karan returned home. He didn't speak a word to her and straight away went to his room.

"No matter Mr. Husband. I am going to make this evening very special for us," she thought. *"Why has the cake and the gift not arrived yet?"*

The doorbell rang. She ran to open the door. She was excited to get the cake and the gift. There was a man standing at the door with a packet in his hand.

"Are you Mrs. Kavita Sinha? This is for you Ma'am." The man handed over the package to her and left.

Kavita was eager to open the gift and see it once before presenting it to Karan.

"Why does the package seem so light?" thought Kavita. She had ordered for some DVDs for Karan as he loved watching movies.

"Has the shop sent he right thing?" she thought while opening the packet. And when she opened the package, to her utter surprise the packet contained divorce papers.

By then Karan also came out from the bedroom. Kavita didn't know how to react. She looked at Karan with teary eyes and asked,

"What is this Karan? Why? Why do you want divorce?"

"I have already said I can't live with you anymore. So stop this melodrama."

Kavita knew this was the end of their relation. She packed her bag and decided to leave for her parents' home. Their divorce process started and they were sent to the experts for counseling who gave them six months to think over their decision before the final divorce.

"Listen Kavita, I don't need a single day to think over my decision. So, these six months we don't need to stay together. We will meet after six months for our divorce formalities."

Kavita didn't say a word. She quietly returned home.

It's three months now. Karan didn't call her for once. Every morning Kavita woke up with the hope that Karan would come to meet her. Everything would be fine. But her hopes never turned into reality.

18th of February. It's their eleventh anniversary.

Kavita's mother wished her early morning.

"What's the use of wishing me Mom when there is no future of our relation," says Kavita.

But within her mind she prayed, *"God please send my husband back to me"*

She kept waiting throughout the day for Karan to come. Karan didn't come. Instead came a bad news. Karan had met with an accident and had been severely injured. He was hospitalized.

Kavita almost lost her senses. She rushed to the hospital bare-footed. Karan was in the ICU in quite a critical condition. He was unconscious. Kavita was continuously chanting God's name. After nearly 24 hours Karan regained his senses. Unfortunately, the lower part of his body was paralyzed.

The doctors released him. Now the fact was that Karan's parents were quite old and moreover they lived in their hometown. Karan needed someone to take care of him. Hence, Kavita decided to move to his place till he recovered. Karan had no other choice but to let Kavita come to his place.

The next two months Kavita took care of him unconditionally. She nursed him like a mother. She did everything possible to cure Karan's paralysis. She visited every doctor, gave every kind of medication and physiotherapy to cure him. She also performed a number of 'pujas' for his well-being.

After 2months of rigorous toil and nursing, finally Karan could move his legs. Eventually, he started with baby footsteps and very soon he was able to stand and walk without any support. The doctors were stunned by such fast recovery. They appreciated Kavita for her efforts. But, Karan was silent.

As Karan recovered, Kavita returned to her parents' home. After she was gone Karan started realizing Kavita's goodness. He started missing her.

"Am I falling for her?" thought Karan. But he somehow suppressed his emotions. And then came the day of their divorce.

Both Karan and Kavita were at the court. Karan was perplexed. He could not understand whether he was taking the right decision. Kavita was still silent. She didn't say a word.

Their names were then called. Kavita got up to get into the chamber, when suddenly there was Karan kneeling down before her.

"Kavita, I don't know how to apologize to you. But I am genuinely ashamed of my behavior. I had created a very wrong impression about you. But now I know

no one can be my better half other than you. Please forgive me and give me a chance to start fresh with you. I promise never to hurt you again."

As Kavita heard all these, tears rolled out of her eyes. She had been waiting for this day since long.

"I too promise to change myself the way you want Karan. I love you a lot. And love is all about understanding each other's likes and dislikes and respecting each other. Let's begin a new chapter of our life." Said Kavita.

"I love you too, my sweetheart."

They finally declared in the court that they don't want to be divorced.

It was a fresh start of an old relation but with a lot of love and respect for each other.

****

Priyanka Bhattacharjee

APARAJITA- THE DEFEAT OF THE UNDEFEATED

Born to a well- to-do family, Aparajita was the only child of her parents. She had everything in her life. She would have been the luckiest girl to be born on Earth, had she had her mother. Unfortunately, her mother died when she was just a toddler. She could never feel the warmth of mother's love.

But, she had her Daddy. And she loved him a lot. However, her father Mr. Anirban Banerjee, a renowned businessman; barely had any time for the little girl. She craved for her Dad's love but failed to get it ever.

Years passed. Aparajita was a teenager. She had started going to college. She had everything in her life. Every luxury that one could ask for. Her father had always fulfilled all her wishes. But, what she really wished for was her father's affection. She wanted to spend time with him, share her feelings with him. She wanted to express how much she missed him. But Mr. Banerjee never had time for her.

Days passed into months and with every passing day Aparajita was being pushed to the darkness of her loneliness till the time she found the love of her life. Her life changed the moment Joy came into her life.

Just like his name, he filled her life with joy and happiness. For the first time she felt what love is.

Till then, she had only read about this indescribable feeling in love stories. But now, it was for real. She couldn't believe that finally she had someone in her life who was genuinely concerned about her. She was in the seventh heaven. The only song that kept on playing in her mind was:

Aaj main upar, aasmaan niche

Aaj main aage, zamaana Hain piche.

Life seemed beautiful with Joy. He was from a middle-class family. Nevertheless, it made no difference in her fondness for him. She was now just waiting for the perfect timing to talk to her father about Joy. Her birthday was in a week's time and she thought it to be the best day to tell her Daddy about their relationship.

Like any other year, this year too her Daddy threw a grand party on his daughter's birthday. Early that morning Anirbaan went to his daughter's room to wish her. She was in deep sleep. Gently, he caressed her cheeks and kissed her.

As she opened her eyes, Anirbaan affectionately wished her,

"Happy Birthday, my child. I know, I can hardly give you any time. But it's all because I want to give you every happiness of the world."

"I understand Daddy." Aparajita replied. *"But my real happiness is to be with you."*

Anirbaan promised to give her time. He then said,

"I have thrown a party this evening for your birthday as usual. But there's something special. I have a surprise for you."

"O Daddy! Truly." Aparajita was excited. *"I too have a surprise for you."*

"That's great. Now get up my sweetheart and get ready for the evening."

Aparajita happiness was beyond words. She had barely seen her father in such a jolly mood. She was certain that this was the best day to tell her Dad about Joy.

It was evening. Aparajita's house was packed with guests. Among all the hustle- bustle came down Aparajita clad in a pink gown. She was looking no less than a celestial maiden who had come down from Heaven. As she came downstairs, her eyes were looking for her Dad. She didn't want to waste time anymore. The moment she caught sight of him, she walked up to him and called him up.

"Daddy, I want to share something with you."

But Mr. Banerjee didn't give an ear to what she was trying to say. Instead, he told her,

"Come with me. I have an announcement to make. The surprise I said about in the morning."

And in an elated tone, to the utter surprise of Aparajita, Anirbaan announced her engagement to the son of one of his business partners. The hall rang with the sound of loud claps and amidst such applause stood Aparajita startled. She couldn't speak a word. She didn't know what to say.

The party was over. Anirbaan was extremely delighted. Finally, Aparajita gathered her courage and approached her Dad.

"Daddy I have something to say."

She then told her father about Joy. Anirbaan got mad in rage. He was no way ready to accept Joy as his son-in-law. After a lot of pleading and begging, finally Anirbaan agreed to meet Joy. Aparajita called Joy and asked him to come to their home to meet her father the next day.

That night, Aparajita could not sleep. She was both excited and nervous. She just prayed to God that everything goes smoothly between Joy and her father.

The next day Joy was to come at 10 in the morning. Aparajita was waiting eagerly for him to come. Her father, Anirbaan was also at home. The clock struck 10. Aparajita's heart was beating fast. It was 10:15. Joy hadn't arrived yet. She was standing at the door waiting for her love to come. But, he was nowhere to be seen. It was 11:30 now. Anirbaan remarked,

"Your love doesn't have the courage to face the reality. He was playing with your emotions. He will never come."

But, Aparajita could not accept this. She knew Joy could never betray her. He, definitely, must be in some trouble. She took her mobile to make a call when her phone rang. She could see Joy's name flashing on the screen. Instantly she picked up the call.

"Hello! Where are you Joy? Dad is waiting for you. Come soon."

A trembling voice spoke from the other side.

"H...he...hello Apaa... hello Aparajita, I am Abir. Joy's friend. Joy met with an accident. He has left us forever."

The mobile fell from her hand. Aparajita fainted. When she got back to her senses she burst out into tears. She couldn't believe it. Once again, she lost love in her life. Bereaved in her grief, Aparajita was once again left in her lonely world.

Two years went by. Aparajita was now married to the man her father chose for her. He was just as busy as Anirbaan. A rich businessman who could give everything to his wife except his love and time. She yearned for his love and attention. But, never got it.

Ten years passed. Aparajita was now a mother of an eight years old girl. She loved her daughter a lot. She named her daughter Amod meaning pleasure. Truly her pleasure in life now was her daughter. She wanted to fill Amod's life with all that she was deprived of. She knew her daughter too didn't get her father's attention. Therefore, she tried to fill the deficit.

She was happy with her daughter. But, somewhere still she craved for true love. For someone who would understand her, love her, give her the shoulder to rest her head on.

It was a mid-June afternoon. Aparajita was not well. She was suffering from high fever. Her husband was not in town. There was nobody to take care of her. As Amod returned from school, she saw her mother lying in bed unconscious. Her body was blazing in high temperature. She didn't know what to do. Suddenly, she came up with an idea to call her Tuition teacher Shaswat.

Shaswat was a young lad in his twenties. He used to take private tuitions and was looking for a job. He used to come to Aparajita's home to teach Amod. But, never did Aparajita and Shaswat talk to each other.

However, as soon as Amod called him; a kind soul he was, he ran to their rescue. He called for a doctor who then prescribed some medicines. Aparajita took time to recover. She had weakened. It was more of her mental illness than physical. Nonetheless, during her illness, Shaswat took a lot of care as her husband was not there.

Gradually, they started talking to each other and in no time they became good friends. They started sharing all their feelings with each other. Aparajita started enjoying his company. And Shaswat too liked being with her. They would talk for hours and never got bored. Aparajita slowly realized that she had started falling for Shaswat and she was certain that he too was no different. Life once more seemed to be colorful to her. She woke up wanting to live again.

One evening as Shaswat came to take Amod's class, Aparajita noticed that he seemed distressed. After the class, Aparajita asked him what the matter was. But Shaswat hesitated to say anything. On being insisted again and again, he finally told her that his mother was suffering from cancer and he now needed a lot of money for her treatment. He was unable to arrange such a big amount.

Aparajita consoled him saying, *"Don't worry Shaswat. I shall give you the amount."*

"No, Ma'am. How can I take from you?"

"Take it as a loan and return it back when you get a good job. Now go home and relax."

Shaswat left. Aparajita thought, *"Tomorrow when I give him the money, I shall tell him about my feelings. He too loves me. It's time we admit it to each other."*

The next day Aparajita was very excited. She was chirping around waiting for Shaswat to come. Shaswat used to come at 3 in the evening for Amod's classes. It seemed the time was not passing. After a wait for an eternity, finally Shaswat came. Aparajita waited for the class to be over.

After the class, Aparajita came down to the hall with the money and handed it to Shaswat.

"Shaswat, I have something to say."

But, before she could speak a word, Shaswat caught hold of her hands. He was in tears. He knelt before her.

"I have no words to express my gratefulness to you. I have always thought you as my elder sister. And you really supported me as such. I shall owe my mother's life to you forever."

Aparajita was speechless. She went upstairs to her room without speaking a word. Shaswat couldn't understand what had happened.

Aparajita was in tears. Her heart was broken once again. She vowed never to speak to Shaswat. Amod then came to the room looking for her mother.

"Mom, Sir is leaving. He is waiting for you."

Instantaneously, a thought came into her mind.

"Throughout my life, I have craved for love. My soul is hungry for love. And today when I got someone who actually loves me purely, I kicked him off just because he called me his sister. No, I can't let him go. I need to stop him. I did a grave mistake."

At once she ran downstairs just to find that Shaswat had already left. She knew Shaswat was gone never to return. Once more she failed in love.

Aparajita, the undefeated was defeated in love forever.

****

Priyanka Bhattacharjee

THE REALIZATION

Have you ever been crazy about someone? Did you ever feel that infatuation for someone where you only dream of the person and want to have him in your life by any means? And how would you feel if that person comes into your life willingly? Sravya had such an experience. Let's find out what happened when Mohit, her craze came into her life.

Sravya was in the seventh heaven. The boy of her dreams, Mohit, who had always been a part of her imagination proposed her. What more could she ask for?

Sravya caught the first glimpse of Mohit on the very first day of her college. As she entered the college premise, she saw a handsome, dashing young boy in a red t-shirt and blue denims standing at the gate along with his friends. The moment she saw him; she couldn't take her eyes off his face. He was her dream man. The one she had been waiting for since long.

Mohit noticed Sravya glancing at him constantly. He gave her a smile. She couldn't stop giggling. Later that day Mohit called her. He was in his third year. As seniors his group was calling the freshers for their amusement.

"What's your name?"

Priyanka Bhattacharjee

"Sravya," she replied.

Mohit asked her few more questions which she replied to. But, all the while she just kept looking at his face. She was carried away by the aura of Mohit's persona.

All the way home she kept talking about Mohit to her best friend Rashi.

"You know, there is some kind of magic in this guy. I am just crazy about him. Only if I could have him in my life, Rashi."

"Forget it," Rashi replied. *"He is the son of one of the richest businessman in our town. Thousands of girls are mad after him. Do you think he would ever even think about you?"*

"There may be thousands but none like me. You never know, if I would be the one," replied Sravya confidently.

That night Sravya could not sleep. She just kept thinking about Mohit. If love at first sight really exists, Sravya felt this was it. She had fallen for him.

Everyday she would look for opportunities to meet him, talk to him once. Eventually they turned into friends. Sravya would make his favorite dishes and take for him to college. She did everything that Mohit liked just to impress him.

And then came the day, Sravya had been waiting for since long. Mohit proposed her. That too in Bollywood style. She always dreamt of a handsome lad in her life who would propose her with chocolates, roses, balloons and teddies. And she could see her dream turn into reality. She couldn't wait to say yes.

She just cried out, "*I love you. Yes, I do. More than anybody on this Earth.*"

Sravya's life was filled with romance now. Her day started with Mohit's phone call and ended in his thoughts.

Four months passed since they started dating. Sravya's life was just like a Yash Chopra movie. She had the hero of her life. What more did she need? She was the envy of every girl in her college. However, her parents were completely in the dark about her affair. Sravya didn't say anything about Mohit to them. Once she even thought to, but Mohit stopped her from doing so.

17th July: it was Mohit's birthday. He invited all his friends to a private party that he had thrown at his new flat which his father gifted him on his birthday. Sravya was also invited. Sravya lied at her home saying she was going to her friend's place for night stay. They had a blast at Mohit's flat. Food, drinks everything was in abundance. It was the first time Sravya had tasted alcohol and she was almost out of her senses. At around midnight all his friends left. Now Sravya and Mohit were alone in the flat.

Sravya was completely drunk. She was in Mohit's arms. Both came closer. That was a weak moment. He leaned forward and kissed her passionately and she too kissed him back more fervently than ever before. Sravya submitted herself to Mohit. She loved him and blindly trusted him.

"Mohit you are the only one whom I want to entrust with my days and nights. I want to be yours both physically and emotionally." Sravya said.

She hugged him tight. Mohit too embraced her and said,

"If you truly love me, just be mine without any hesitation. Let's cross every barrier tonight. Let's be one."

Sravya had no reason to hesitate. They were in love. She could feel Mohit's hands slowly going into her curly hair. She began enjoying the moment. She tightly held Mohit's gorgeous male body against hers and dived into his masculine smell. As they continued kissing each other, Mohit's hands kept moving all over her body and Sravya didn't even attempt to stop him. They rolled into the bed like a snowball and they were lost in the world of love and lust.

The night passed and as the day dawned and Sravya opened her eyes, she found herself in Mohit's arms. She looked at Mohit's face who was still sleeping and breathed a sigh of relief. She kissed him on his forehead and just whispered,

"You complete me Mohit. I am yours forever. Thank you for being in my life."

Mohit opened his eyes and left the bed in rush.

"Hurry up Sravya. We need to go."

Mohit dropped her at her home and left. Sravya rang the doorbell. Her mother opened the door.

"Where were you? Why are you so late? I called Richa. She told me you were not there. Where did you spend the night?"

But Sravya was in her own world. She didn't bother to hear what her mother was saying.

A week passed since then. Surprisingly, in these seven days there was no news of Mohit. He was not in the college. Nor did he call Sravya even for once. Every time Sravya called she could just hear,

"The number you are calling is currently switched off. Please try after some time."

Sravya had no clue of what was going on. She was very worried. She didn't know whom to ask. Finally, she called his best friend Abhi,

"Abhi, can you please tell me where Mohit is? It's almost fifteen days and I haven't got any news of him. Is he fine?"

"Yes, absolutely. Didn't he tell you that he is going to London for his higher studies? That's why he had thrown such a grand party for all his friends."

Sravya was shocked. *"London! He didn't say me anything. And wasn't the party for his birthday?"*

"Birthday! Hey silly girl, Mohit's birthday is on the 21st of January. So, he fooled you too."

"Fooled me! Why will he? I am his girlfriend."

"Girlfriend! Haha! Miss Sravya, let me tell you Mohit has no girlfriend. He plays with girls. He played with you too. And now he is done with you. So forget him."

Abhi disconnected the call. Sravya couldn't believe what she heard. How could Mohit do this to her? She loved him madly. And now she couldn't bear this betrayal.

She was totally broken. She left going to college. Neither did she eat nor sleep. She stopped talking to everyone at home. Just kept on crying. It's now that her parents came to know everything from Richa. They tried their best to console her but all in vain. She was sunk in depression. They consulted a number of doctors but nothing seemed to work. It seemed as if Sravya had lost her hope to live.

One morning as Sravya's mother entered her room to wake her up, she gave a huge cry. Her father immediately ran to her room. Sravya was lying unconscious on her bed. Blood was dripping from her wrist. Sravya had attempted suicide. They immediately rushed her to the hospital.

She was taken to the emergency ward immediately.

The nurse said to her mother in a consoling tone, *"Don't worry. A very good doctor has joined our hospital. I am sure he will save your daughter."*

"Who's the patient? What happened nurse?" Asked the doctor when suddenly his eyes fell on Sravya's parents.

"Aunty! Uncle! What happened? Why are you both here?"

"Amit. Beta save our daughter. She has attempted suicide."

Amit was Sravya's childhood friend whom she always neglected because he was not good-looking or rather didn't meet the criteria of Sravya's definition of being handsome. Nonetheless, Amit had always loved Sravya.

"Don't worry, Aunty. Uncle relax. Sravya will be absolutely fine."

Saying this Amit went inside. And after a few hours came out. Sravya was out of danger then. Her parents thanked Amit.

Sravya was now better and was released from the hospital. But, she was still in the same condition. Her parents were very worried. They didn't understand how they could get back their chirpy, fun- loving Sravya back. They were helpless. Finally, they decided to take Amit's help. Possibly he could do some miracle.

Priyanka Bhattacharjee

Amit came to their home in the evening. He straightaway went to Sravya's room.

"How are you Sravya?" She was shocked to see Amit after so many years. She didn't even know that it was Amit who saved her life.

As soon as she saw him she burst into tears. She told him everything.

"I was such a fool, Amit. How could I love someone blindly? I have ruined my life. Now I can't live without him."

"Stop acting like an idiot, Sravya. Life doesn't stop for anyone. You have your parents. Think about them. You cannot end your life for someone who didn't even value you. There are so many people around you who love you unconditionally. Just try to recognize them."

Amit's words had a strange spell on her. She slowly started recovering. Within a span of a month, Sravya returned back to her normal life. She apologized to her parents for all her mistakes. She realized the practicality of life.

Five years down the incident. Sravya completed her graduation and was engaged in a job. She was now quite a matured lady. She knew the practicality of life. Amit was now a very good friend of hers. She shared everything with him.

One evening Amit invited her for dinner. They both went to a restaurant where he proposed her.

Priyanka Bhattacharjee

"Sravya, I don't know any filmy dialogues. I don't know how to impress girls. I don't know whether I fit in your definition of a lover. But the only thing I know is that I love you unconditionally. I may not give you roses. I may not give you gifts everyday. But I promise to give you limitless love. Will you be mine? Will you marry me, Sravya?"

Sravya was dumbstruck. She remained quiet for a while and then just nodded her head to give her consent. She was speechless.

Soon, their engagement was announced. Their engagement was not a grand celebration. A few friends and relatives were invited. Both Amit and Sravya didn't want their day to be a pompous show.

Just as the ceremony was about to begin, a car stopped at their door and someone got down from it. To Sravya's amazement, the one who got down was none other than Mohit. Sravya didn't know how to react. The most unfortunate chapter of her life which she had torn apart was standing in front of her.

Mohit knelt down before Sravya with tears in his eyes.

"I am sorry Sravya. Please forgive me. I broke your heart. But I have now realized my mistake. I want you back in my life. Please don't get engaged to anyone else. Give me a chance to reform."

Sravya was silent. She looked at Mohit and then turned towards Amit who was standing there without least expectation on his face. After a while Sravya spoke:

"I am happy Mohit you realized your mistake. The man whom I loved with my heart and my soul is today at my feet asking for forgiveness. I do forgive you because I loved you. It's great you realized how much you had hurt me."

"Thankyou Sravya. I promise to give you every happiness."

"Wait Mohit. I haven't completed. Just like you realized your mistake, I too realized mine. I always ran after good looks and couldn't **see one's** *heart. Your looks impressed me and I got crazy about you. But Amit made me realize that we should judge a person by his heart and not his looks. Amit may not be as handsome as you, but his heart is as vast as a sea which is filled with immense love. You broke your promise. You betrayed me. If I too do the same what would be the difference. I can never cheat the one who gave me a new life. Sorry Mohit. But I don't love you anymore. I love Amit. And I would be his forever."*

Mohit left the venue ashamed. Amit and Sravya got engaged and now they are happily married with two daughters.

****

Priyanka Bhattacharjee

WITH YOU OR WITHOUT YOU

Today she feels like a free bird. After years of being caged, she can today breathe the air of liberty. She went to a nearby park and sat on a bench there. Life was never the same for her five years back.

Aahana, a girl of 23; had just graduated in Mass-communication and had millions of dreams in her eyes. She wanted to make her career in journalism. She wanted to be a strong pillar of her family. Her father always wished to have a son and she desired to be the one for him.

But, destiny had other plans. Her parents were looking for a suitable groom for her. They wanted her to be married at the earliest. She pleaded with them. But neither her father nor her mother gave an ear to her pleas. Finally, she knelt down to their will and gave her consent for marriage.

In a month's time, Aahana got married to Prateek who worked in a multinational company. He had his parents and a younger sister in the family. Life seemed beautiful after marriage and Aahana felt that her parents had taken the right decision.

She found Prateek to be a decent guy. He too loved her a lot and took care of her. Everyone in the family were affectionate towards her.

For a year everything went on smoothly. A career oriented woman as she was, turned out to be a devoted housewife. She sacrificed all her dreams for the sake of her family. She was glad to be a homemaker who was loved limitlessly by her husband. Her life couldn't have been better than this.

It was her first wedding anniversary. She had been waiting eagerly for this day. She made a lot of preparation for this day. In the evening she decked up in the best of her outfit just like a bride. Now, she just waited for her husband to return. Prateek usually returned at 7 in the evening. It was 6:30. Aahana was anxiously waiting for Prateek. She had so many surprises for him.

Time kept ticking. It was 7:30 and Prateek didn't reach home.

"*He might be busy in his work*", thought Aahana.

She once thought of calling him. But, then decided to wait. Time kept passing but there was no sign of Prateek. Aahana keenly looked towards the entrance with the hope that Prateek would return but in despair.

It was already midnight. Eventually, Prateek reached home. However, much to Aahana's surprise, Prateek was not in his senses. He was drunk. Aahana was shocked to see this. All her expectations splintered like fragments of glass. She couldn't believe that Prateek didn't remember their first anniversary and came home sloshed. She somehow managed to take him to bed. That night, she couldn't sleep.

The next morning Aahana thought that Prateek would have realized his mistake and would come up to her to apologize for what he had done. Surprisingly, nothing as such happened. Prateek had no regrets. Infact, he didn't even care to ask Aahana why she looked upset. He had his breakfast and left for office. Aahana stood there wordless trying to understand the new Prateek.

Once again destiny played its game and life took its turn. Prateek was no more the person whom Aahana knew a year ago. He had completely changed. He didn't bother to ask about his wife's wellbeing. He started coming home late. He also took to excessive drinking.

Aahana's life turned into hell. She had to face all kinds of domestic violence. She tried to keep a lot of patience with the hope that someday Prateek would change. But, nothing changed. She tried to talk to her in-laws. But, they instead of teaching their son a lesson kept blaming her. She was left helpless.

But even after so much of agony, Aahana never thought to leave her home. She bore every torment silently. She couldn't understand the reason behind Prateek's inhumane behavior.

She thought to talk to Prateek. She didn't want her beautiful bond to break. That evening she cooked all his favorite dishes. She decorated the room with candles and flowers. She wanted to rekindle the romance between them.

It was Aahana's good luck that evening that Prateek came home early and he was not even drunk. Aahana was overwhelmed at this. As Prateek entered the house, she ran to him and held him tightly.

Prateek was also surprised to see his home all decorated with flowers and candles. He asked Aahana,

"Is there anything special today?"

"Every moment you are with me makes it special Prateek. I love you a lot. Can't we start over again? I don't know what's missing in our relation. But, let's find it out and be happy together forever."

Prateek sat silent listening to Aahana. He spoke not a word. Just held Aahana's hands in his. She understood Prateek had realized his mistake. That night was special for Aahana. She got back her love. She just desired to lose herself in his arms.

Two years passed since then. Aahana was the mother of a beautiful baby girl. She had one complete family. Her life surrounded around her husband and her child. What was bygone was gone forever. She prayed and thanked God for all she had in her life.

But, she never knew how instantly her life was to change. That morning as Prateek was getting ready for his office, suddenly his phone rang. Prateek went out to take the call. Aahana didn't notice as she always saw Prateek engaged in official calls. After a while he came inside and told Aahana that he urgently needs to go to Mumbai for some business meeting. Aahana instantly did all his packing and he left in an hour.

After Prateek left, she got back to her household chores. While she was feeding her baby, her phone rang. She picked it up. It was her school friend Richa.

"Hey Aahana! Where are you? And where's Prateek?"

"I am at my home and Prateek has gone to Mumbai today for his business meeting. But what's the matter?" Surprised Aahana asked.

Hesitantly Richa said, *"Aahana, your husband is lying. He is here in Delhi. I have seen him here in Hotel Plaza and he was not alone. There was a young lady with him."*

Aahana couldn't believe what she heard. She couldn't imagine even in her dreams that Prateek could cheat on her. On being insisted by Richa, she agreed to go to the hotel and see with her own eyes.

She booked a cab and carrying her child in her arms she went to Hotel Plaza. All the way she just prayed that whatever Richa told her would be her misconception. On reaching the hotel, she got off the car and there Richa was waiting for her.

Richa took the baby from her and said, "Go check for yourself. Your husband is in room number 1108."

Aahana pulled herself together and went to the reception to ask who occupied 1108. But, they refused to answer. She somehow had to find the truth. Therefore, she decided to wait there till they come out. She asked Richa to take her daughter and go to her home. Richa left while she waited to find out the truth. All the while she just kept her fingers crossed.

Finally, after a long wait of two hours, she decided to return.

"How stupid I am. I shouldn't have come into Richa's words. How can I doubt the person who loves me unconditionally?"

Just as Aahana got up to leave, the door of the elevator opened and out came Prateek holding the hand of a beautiful young lady whom Prateek had once introduced to her as his colleague.

Aahana was shocked. She couldn't believe her eyes. The one whom she blindly trusted, the one for whom she sacrificed all her dreams, the one who was her life- was cheating on her. She was shattered. Her heart was broken into pieces. Her life flashed in front of her eyes in a moment.

How could someone be so selfish? How could he do this to her? Where would she go now?

Several questions arose in her mind. She had a baby daughter. But, now she couldn't remain silent anymore. She couldn't silently bear his infidelity.

She wiped her tears and walked up straight to Prateek.

Prateek was shocked to see Aahana there. But before he could say anything, Aahana slapped him on his face.

"People like you deserve nothing better than this."

Prateek stood there ashamed and Aahana returned to the house once she called her home. She packed her bag, took her child and left Prateek's home never to return.

In a short span of time, she sent him divorce notice. Prateek came to her apologizing for his mistake. But, this time there was nothing that could erase his betrayal. She was determined about what she wanted from life now. In a span of a year they got divorced.

As she sat in the park, these five years of her life flashed before her. Till now she lived for others' happiness. She sacrificed all her dreams to fulfill others' will. But, now it's her time. She will live for herself and her daughter. She got up from the bench, took a deep breath and walked out of the park to begin her new journey. A journey where she would decide what her destination would be.

She got the biggest lesson of life. Love is truly the greatest gift of God to mankind. Nonetheless, love doesn't mean only sacrificing your dreams and happiness for others. It's equally important to love oneself. ******************

Priyanka Bhattacharjee

THE UNDEFINING STRING OF LOVE

"Hello. Am I speaking to Lakshita? Did you give an advertisement in the newspaper regarding a roommate?"

That one phone call and my whole life changed. Never did I think that the sweet voice calling me from the other end of the phone would become such an inseparable part of my life.

Well, let me introduce myself. I am Lakshita- a small town girl. But, just like my name I had a lot of high aspirations and that's why after my graduation I shifted to Delhi for my higher studies. I completed my studies in Mass Communication under Delhi University. And just in a couple of months I got the job to assist the senior editor of a leading magazine.

Life was running quite smoothly. I could see my dreams gradually turning into reality. Everything was perfect except a strange loneliness that had engulfed my life. Delhi had given me everything that I always wanted in my life. A degree from a well-known university, a good job and a couple of good friends who always stand by me during thick and thin.

But, there was something more that I craved for. True love. Yet, I never got attracted to any man ever. Strangely, I could never find the reason. Friends I had many- I used to go out and chill with them, have fun and booze together. But, that romantic feel I never had for anyone. I even tried to get into one or two relations but failed badly. Maybe 'LOVE' is not my cup of tea. I am not like other girls. I don't enjoy all kinds of girlish talks. Somewhat tomboy kind of, you know. Probably, that could be a reason. Hence, at the end of the day I am left lonely in my flat. Nobody to talk to or share with what I feel.

One day, my colleague Sheena came up with a wonderful idea.

"Hey Lakshita, why don't you share your flat with someone. There are many who look for shared flats to live. That way you will have a company and also all your expenses would get shared."

I found the idea excellent. I talked to my landlord who had no issues till the tenant is a female and I don't let more than two roommates in the flat. At once I gave an advertisement in a local daily. Soon I began getting a number of phone calls. But, for one reason or the other I couldn't find a perfect mate to share my roommate.

And then that phone call which actually changed my life. It was Sunday and the voice I heard over the phone strangely attracted me. I called her to my place for a meeting. I can't explain but I wanted to meet that person who had such an appealing voice.

She said she would come to meet me at 4 in the evening. I kept waiting till the doorbell rang sharp at 4. The doorbell confirmed one thing- she's punctual. Quite contradictory to my nature. I went and opened the door and there stood a girl as sweet as her voice. In a yellow salwar suit and long hair she looked like a fairy from heaven. I couldn't move my eyes from her.

"Hello, I am Hrishita. I called you in the morning regarding the advertisement."

Her voice brought me back to senses. I felt embarrassed. (How could I look at a girl in this way?)

"Hi. Please come in. I am Lakshita. Nice to meet you."

"It's same here." She replied.

We talked for a long time and discussed on all the aspects. A girl of 23, she was from Meerut and had recently joined a corporate office in Delhi as an office executive. After all our discussion, it was decided that she would shift into my flat the next day. I kept thinking about her after she left. She was totally different from me. Will we be able to adjust with each other? However, I was now happy that I would no more be alone in the flat. But, one question that kept disturbing me all throughout the night was that what it was that strangely attracted me towards her.

The next day she shifted into my flat early in the morning even before I left for office. I was already late for office. Hence, I just handed over the extra key of the flat to her and hurried off to office. But, before leaving I couldn't stop myself from taking a quick glance of her. She was a real definition of beauty.

My day in office was quite a busy one. But, I was waiting eagerly to go home that day. For the first time there was someone at home to open the door for me. First time I would not be alone at home. Finally, I reached home at 8:30 PM and as expected she was there to open the door for me. And as she opened the door, I kept staring at her. She was an embodiment of eternal beauty.

"Welcome home Lakshita." She said with a smile.

I was embarrassed once again. It was strange I kept glancing at her all the time.

I had taken home a bottle of wine to celebrate the day when I had a new partner to share my flat with. After taking a quick shower I asked Hrishita to join me for a glass of wine. But, the kind of girl she was, she politely refused me.

"I am sorry but I don't drink. But, I don't mind giving you company."

Her words were so sweet that they could easily melt anyone's heart. As said, she sat with me as I was having my wine. We had long conversation and she told me about all her struggles.

"I come from an orthodox family where girls are never encouraged to move ahead in life. But, I had my dreams. I didn't want to get married so early. I

wanted to stand on my feet. I wanted to be established in life. But, my family never supported me. They tortured me a lot and forcibly tried to get me married to an aged landlord. I escaped from my home on my wedding night and today I am here struggling to make my identity."

Her words brought tears to my eyes. But I was also inspired by her story.

"You are such a brave soul, Hrishita. You are an inspiration for every girl who wants to prove herself and stand against the social norms. My heart is filled with respect for you and now onwards I will always be there for your help."

That night onwards we became best of friends. My life became so better with her. Now, I don't feel lonely after returning home. In fact, our evenings after returning home from our respective works would be filled with interesting conversations and good food (as Hrishita was an excellent cook) and on weekends we would usually go out for long drives and have a lot of fun.

Days rolled on in a blink of an eye and we didn't even realise when it had already been six months of us staying together. In these six months, our bond became very strong. But, I didn't realise that it was more than just mere friendship till the unfortunate night of 25 December.

It being Christmas night, I had a get- together in my office and therefore I was late than usual in reaching home. To my surprise, the door was locked which meant Hrishita was not at home. In these six months of us living together, this never happened. Hrishita was always the first one to reach home. But that day it was 10:30 at night and she was still not there. However, I wasn't much worried as it was Christmas and probably they too had celebration at their office.

I freshened up and sat in the balcony waiting for Hrishita to come. But, it was midnight now and Hrishita was yet not home. I was worried. What could be the reason? The kind of girl she was; she couldn't be so late. As I was thinking what to do, my phone started ringing. It was Hrishita's call. I picked up the call at once. But, it was not Hrishita.

"Hello. My name is Harish and I am calling from City Hospital."

"Hello. Where is Hrishita? Why are you calling from her phone?"

"Actually, the one who owns this phone had a serious accident and I brought her to hospital. Yours was the last dialed number in her call log. So, I called you. Please come soon"

This news shattered me. I ran to the hospital in no time. Hrishita's condition was quite serious. She was badly injured and was under observation in the ICU. I spent the whole night sitting outside the ICU praying for her recovery. But, it seemed as if my prayers were not being heard.

Priyanka Bhattacharjee

It was already 24 hours and Hrishita had yet not regained her consciousness. I was completely broken. I couldn't even imagine in my dreams of losing Hrishita. I was in tears when the nurse came up to me enquiring about Hrishita's family for some formalities. It was now important to inform Hrishita's family about her condition. I took the contact details of Hrishita's family from her office and informed her family. Within a few hours her family was in hospital. Her mother was in tears to see her in that condition. I tried to console her whereas I myself was feeling devastated. It seemed there was no hope of her recovery when all of a sudden the doctor came out:

"Lakshita congratulations. Your friend has regained her consciousness and now she is out of danger. Within a few days she will be completely fine."

These words of the doctor gave me a new life. I ran towards the ICU. As I saw Hrishita in her senses I felt I got the world's best gift. I was the happiest person on earth then. She slowly opened her eyes and smiled at me. That was the moment I realized how important she was for me. It was hard for me accept but the truth was that I had fallen for her. Yes, I was in love. I was in love with Hrishita. And I couldn't think my life without her then onwards.

It was a week and Hrishita was gradually recovering. And these seven days I never left her even for a second. I took leave from my office too. I wanted to be with her constantly and I did so. It is difficult to explain but I was getting more and more attracted towards her.

But, was it normal? How could I be attracted towards a girl in this way?

These thoughts were disturbing me. A constant commotion was going on between my heart and brain. A girl like me who hardly got attracted to a boy had now fallen for a girl. I didn't know whom to share my emotions with. But, one thing I knew for sure was that my feelings were genuine and nothing could stop me from loving her.

Hrishita was much better by then. The doctor gave her discharge but advised her for complete bed rest for the next seven days. Her parents wanted to take her back home. But I was surprised when she refused to go.

No Maa, I don't want to go back home. I am more than happy to have my family back in my life. But, I don't want to go back. I want to stay here with Lakshita, my roommate and my best friend.

I had no idea why she didn't go back home with her family but I was glad that she would be with me. What else could I ask for?

The next day was special for me. Hrishita was to return home. I had to do something special for her. So, before she got discharged, I went home and decorated it for her welcome. Finally, Hrishita was home after ten days. She was overwhelmed to see all the preparations I did to welcome her. She was in tears.

Lakshita, I can't believe. You have done so much for me. No words are enough to thank you. It's because of you that I got my family back. I shall be ever grateful to you.

I was overwhelmed by her words. I wanted to open up my feelings to her. But I knew this was not possible. I couldn't lose her friendship by revealing my love for her. I was happy that we were together.

Days kept passing and Hrishita was completely recovered and was back to her normal life. We both had a busy schedule throughout the week but weekends were meant to have fun. We used to plan short trips during weekends. It was fun being together. Now and then we visited each other's families. By now I was madly in love with this simple small town girl. She was my lifeline. But the saddest part was that I couldn't express my feelings to her. However, one thing was certain. Hrishita loved me too. But, probably not the way I did. I kept looking for opportunities to tell her about my feelings. But couldn't dare to. And then finally destiny made its own way.

It was Saturday night. We both came home early that evening. While returning I bought three bottles of beer. That weekend we had no plans of going out. So, I thought to booze at home. Hrishita as usual refused to have any. She got busy preparing dinner. However, I wanted to booze with her. Hence, I thought of convincing her. After a lot of pleadings, she finally agreed.

Fine, I will give you company but only a few sips. You know Lakshita I have never tried.

It's okay Hrishita. Everything has its first time. Just give it a try. I will not force you if you don't like it.

Hrishita quickly prepared the dinner and then we both sat in our balcony. I lit a few scented candles around and played some soft music to lift the mood. Hrishita was delighted to see all the preparations.

Oh my God Lakshita! This is a perfect date set up. Had you been a boy, I would have fallen for you.

Can't a girl be fallen for? (I quietly murmured.)

She was excited to see everything. I poured a little beer in a glass and offered to her. Hesitatingly, she took the first sip. She didn't like the taste. But after a few sips she started enjoying. And to my utter surprise, within no time she drank a bottle of beer. She was now drunk.

She slowly got up from her place and sat beside me. She held my hands into hers and kept staring at me without blinking for once. There was a deep passion that I could feel in her eyes. I too kept looking at her and then lovingly caressing her hair called her:

"Hrishita, are you fine? Do you want to take some rest?"

I was a little worried about her as it was for the first time ever that she had tasted alcohol.

"I am absolutely fine, Lakshita. But, there's something that I want to tell you."

"Yes, please tell me. What is it?"

"It has been days I wanted to tell you about it but could never muster up the courage. But today I just want to confess my feelings to you. I don't know how you would react after listening to what I say. However, I just don't want to hide my emotions anymore."

"Just speak your mind up, dear. You don't need to overthink."

There was a strange excitement in my mind. I was eager to know what she had to say. There was silence all around and it seemed as if I could hear my heart beat.

"Lakshita, I don't know how and why. I don't know when. But I have started loving you like anything. And it's not the love that exists between friends. It's more than that. I am deeply in love with you. I know this is strange. I know after this moment I shall lose you forever. Nonetheless, I had to admit my feelings to you. I couldn't keep it to myself anymore. I am ready to leave……"

"Just be quiet. You don't need to say anything more"

I put my finger on her lips. I was in the seventh heaven. My happiness knew no bounds. This was the moment I had long been waiting for. I had almost skipped a beat. I gave her a tight hug. It seemed as if the world had paused. We kept hugging each other for a while and then I spoke.

"Hrishita, I can't express how overwhelmed I am at this moment. This was what I wanted to tell you since long, but kept hesitating. You can't imagine how happy I am today. I love you too, my darling. I love you madly."

Once again we hugged each other. She kept looking at my eyes and we didn't even realise when we got engaged in a passionate kiss. That night we sealed our love till eternity.

So, I too had a love story. Life had turned so beautiful with her. Everything seemed to be sorted. We were to be together in every thick and thin. We promised never to leave each other. We were on cloud nine. Our happiness was immeasurable. We didn't care about the world. We had fallen so crazily for each other that didn't realise the upcoming consequences of our relation.

It was not too long that our love was influenced by an evil eye. We were so engaged in our relation that we had forgotten that both of us had our families and they were not going to take our relation so easily. We had to inform our respective families about our relation. But, before we could do so, life had made its own plans.

It was Sunday and we both were sleeping till late. It was 9 AM when suddenly someone rang our doorbell. With sleepy eyes I dragged myself to open the door and to my surprise, it was Hrishita's parents at the door.

"Oh, Uncle and Aunty! Please come in. Such a surprise. It's a pleasure to have you both here. Please take a seat. Let me call Hrishita."

Hrishita jumped in happiness to see her parents. She ran and embraced her mother in joy.

"Ma, Papa- you didn't even inform me about your visit!"

"Aren't you happy to see us, my child?"

"Certainly Ma. I am so elated. But is there any purpose behind your visit? Is everything fine?"

"Yes dear. We are here to share a news with you."

"What is it, Ma?"

"Dear, we wanted to get you married; but you eloped as you had your dreams to achieve. We were hurt yet we forgave you. You did what your heart desired. But, now it's your turn to fulfill our wish. We have fixed your marriage. The family is really a respectable one in our community. Also the boy we chose for you is a gem. He also has a good reputation and a respectable government job. This is an ideal match for you and we want you to get married to him."

"But Ma...."

"We don't want to hear anything more. Pack your bags. I and your Papa are going to visit your uncle's

home. Once we return, three of us will head back to our village."

Tears were rolling down Hrishita's eyes. I too stood there like a rock. I couldn't believe my ears. I couldn't let her go. She's mine. How could I let her get married to someone else? I had to speak up.

"Aunty...."

Before I could say anything, Hrishita pressed my hand tightly urging me to keep a mum. They both left for Hrishita's uncle's place.

"Why Hrishita? Why didn't you let me speak? Will you get married to the groom your parents chose? Can you ever forget me?"

"No, Lakshita. I can never think of anyone else in my life. But it's useless trying to explain my parents. They can never understand our relation. Leave them, nobody existing on this earth can understand what we feel for each other. We have made the biggest blunder."

"No, my love. Love can never be a blunder. We love each other. And love doesn't understand sex, religion caste or community. We haven't committed any sin. So, what are we scared of? Don't worry. Let them come back. I shall talk to your parents."

"No, Lakshita. They will never understand."

Hrishita went crying into her room and locked the door from inside. I didn't know what to do. She was right. It wasn't easy to make others understand our relation. Certainly, our society hasn't advanced to that extent that it would openly accept our relation. I was so engrossed in my thoughts that I didn't notice that it was more than an hour and Hrishita was yet inside her room.

I went and knocked at her door. But, there was no answer. I started calling her but failed to get any response. A strange fear caught me. I began pushing the door with all my strength until the lock broke and got inside.

What I saw was beyond my imagination. I couldn't believe my eyes. Hrishita was there hanging from the fan. I had almost lost my senses. I ran towards her and clung her by her feet.

"Hrishita, why did you do this? I told you I would find a way out. Why didn't you trust me?"

I was left devastated. My world was upside down in a moment. I couldn't believe what I saw in front of my eyes. How could she end her life? How would I live without her? She left me void of all feelings. My hands and feet got numb when suddenly, my eyes fell on a note kept on her desk. I picked it up:

My Love,

I am sorry. I promised never to leave you. But I couldn't keep my promise. I am leaving this world. I don't have the courage to tell my parents about our relation. I am a coward who can never face the reality. I have always run away from the situation. And today also I am doing the same. I am yours and can never get married to anybody else. But, I can't accept this in front of the society. Hence, I am leaving this world. Please forgive me.

Yours forever

Hrishita.

I was shattered. I hid the letter from everyone. It has been a year that Hrishita left me alone and till today I didn't let anyone know about our relation. Probably, this was how our love story had to culminate. I can never have anyone in my life after her. She will always live in my heart and our love will reign till eternity. Our hearts are tied by that string of love which can't be broken by worldly affairs. Love knows only the language of hearts and nothing can ever separate two loving hearts. Not even death...

****

Priyanka Bhattacharjee

~End~

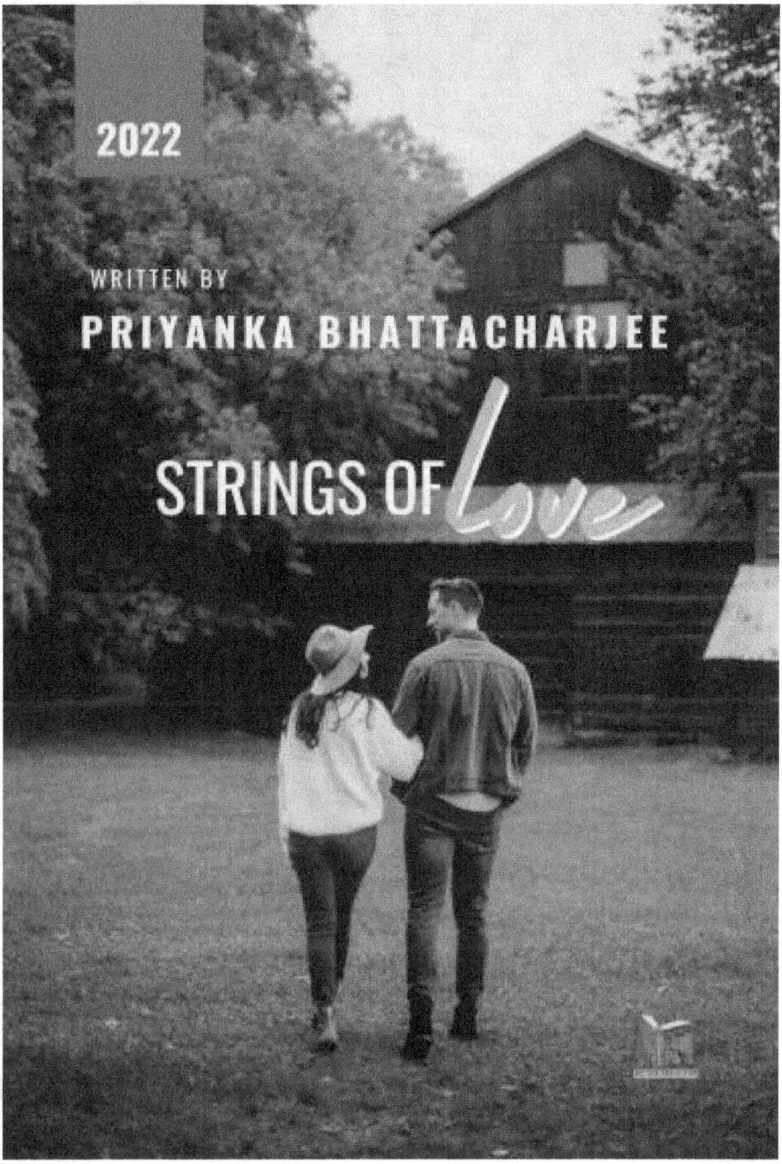
2022
WRITTEN BY
PRIYANKA BHATTACHARJEE
STRINGS OF love

Blurb:

'LOVE' -The most divine feeling that exists on Earth. Infact it is the string of love that ties all of us to eachother. But, we humans at times fail to realise this aesthetic feeling. Sometimes, we don't even realize how and in which form love comes into our life.

'Strings of love' is a book which will give you readers an insight to how important love is in our life. Love is not only about having attraction towards the opposite sex. It's more than that. Love has many forms. With a hope that the essence of love fills all your hearts, the author presents this book to you all.

About the Author:

Priyanka Bhattacharjee who is born and raised in the beautiful land of tea gardens Assam, is an English teacher by profession and has an ardent love for English literature. Having a positive attitude towards life even in the most adverse situations is her sole motto.

Priyanka Bhattacharjee

@noellorenzbooks

www.noellorenz.com

www.ingramcontent.com/pod-product-compliance
Lightning Source LLC
Chambersburg PA
CBHW062113160726
48282CB00026B/783
* 9 7 8 9 3 9 3 6 9 5 0 9 3 *